Diaries
of a
Borderline

BLUE EVERGARDEN

Editing, design, distribution by Bublish
Published by Evergarden's Poetry

eBook ISBN: 978-1-64704-887-7
Paperback ISBN: 978-1-64704-888-4
Hardcover ISBN: 978-1-64704-889-1
Audiobook ISBN: 978-1-64704-890-7

Contents

Part I: Diaries of a Borderline

Part II: This Is Why She Falls Apart

Part III: Leaving Her Mother's Graveyard

Part IV: The Gifts She Found

Part V: The Gifts of Water: The Heart Is How We See Ourselves

Part VI: The Gifts of Earth: A Soul Sprouts

Part VII: The Gifts of Fire: Illuminating the Deeper Mysteries

Part VIII: The Gifts of Air: The Breath of Revelation

Part IX: Letters from beyond the Butterflies

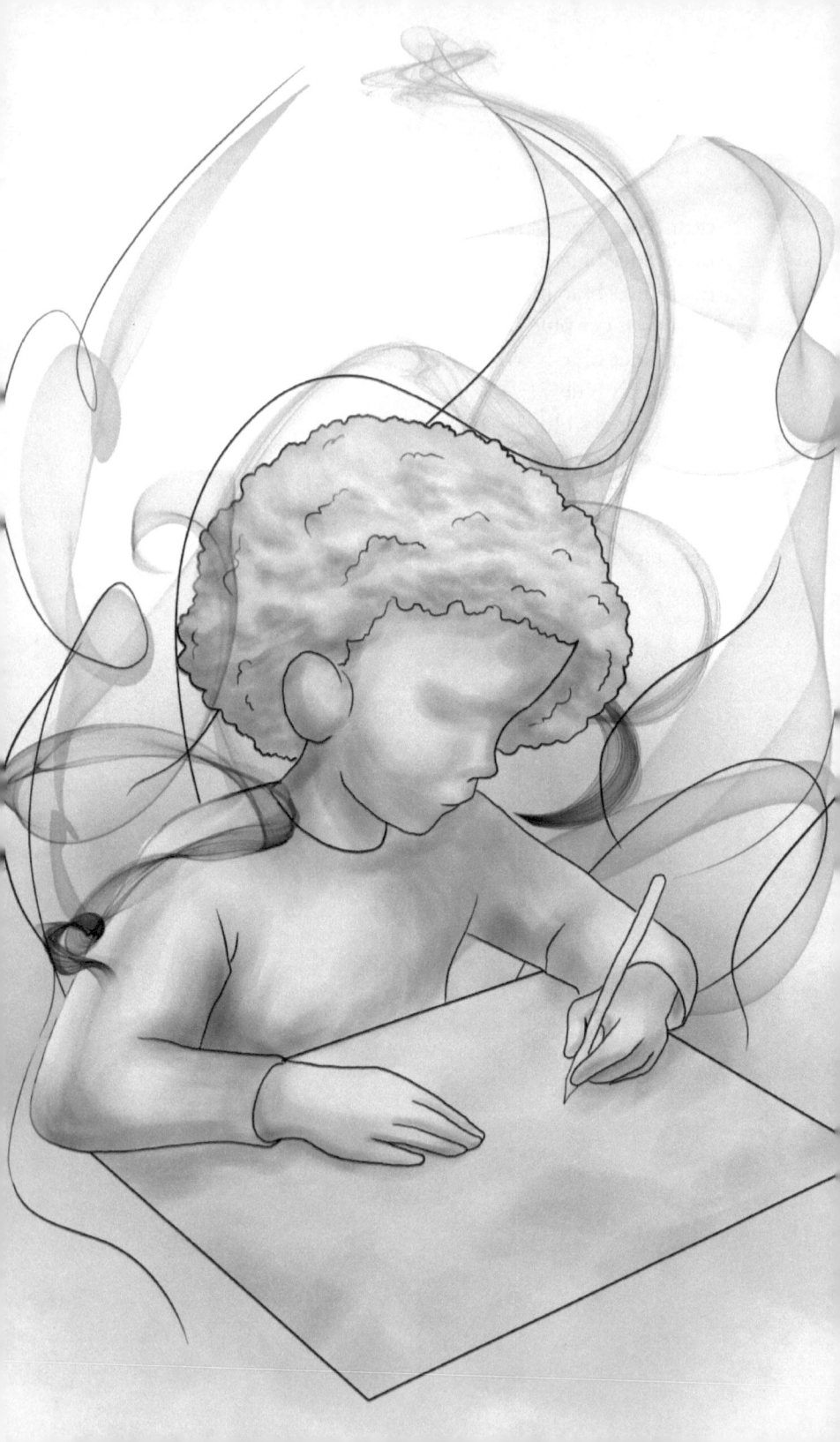

Part I

Diaries of a Borderline

diaries of a borderline i

———————

Still staring at shards of glass on the floor.

She wonders how the fuck she's going to put herself back together now.

She can't remember who she was before the BPD.

Before the cuts.

Before the flashbacks.

Before the dissociation.

Before the guilt.

The loneliness.

The emptiness.

Love isn't enough to heal her heart.

What do you do when the light can't find us anymore?

I try to find the time to confess the signs I'm not fine.

My mind is riddled with reveries disguised as memories.

The voices whisper, "Remember me."

I do.

I do believe in the monsters.

They've always been by my side, guiding love across my wrists.

I can't stop the shadows from strangling the remnants of sunshine hiding the last petals of my soul's rose.

I wish I could be the one my heart loves.

She loves me.

She loves me not.

She hates me.

I wish I didn't hate me more than she did.

More than she did.

Dear Mom,

Was love enough to absolve you?

Did the light finally fill your chest when you gave up the ghost?

Still staring at shards of stars staining her bathroom floor, she wipes the magick from her eyes and looks in the mirror.

A ritual she is all too used to.

They say the eyes are a window to the soul.

She's empty.

The monsters already reaped her joy.

Her hope.

She's drowning in disappointment.

They believe her smile.

The help she needs, she'll never get again.

No closure comes from the dead.

If she could do it all again,

she wouldn't.

Life is learning when the darkness takes,

it never gives it back.

Still staring at shards of sunshine making their way into her bathroom window, she cuts a smile into her face.

It hurts to be happy without them.

What do we do with the wishes life never fulfills?

diaries of a borderline ii

_____

She doesn't sleep.

Reveries haunt her dreams, dying to find the love
she lost to time.

Her nightmares are her happily ever afters.

It's 3:00 a.m. and she's dead awake, wondering if the moonlight
will find her.

It's her fault she's dying on her bedroom floor.

She's sorry she can't love her wounds whole.

She's sorry she still finds herself lost in razor blades and empty
graveyards.

She doesn't know what "I love you" means.

She pours her soul into her cracks, wondering if she can rescue
herself from the monsters she calls Mom.

She doesn't know who she is anymore.

Her scars bloom the roses left at her mom's wake.

She misses her.

diaries of a borderline iii

She wears discomfort on her sleeves.

She hides more than she's letting on.

She dreams of fields of magenta swaying in autumn's wind just before the first snow.

Her breath is hot like a desert.

She sees these mirages appear like ghosts.

She wears discomfort on her sleeves.

These menacing phantoms smile in her shadow.

Their voices discombobulate her.

She gets dizzy when the thoughts get loud.

She can't find her bearings when the magenta fields turn to bone, and she's left staring into her broken reflection, daydreaming of a dreamland she'll never know.

The monsters swathe the fields of grain, seeding her hope to her heart.

She holds the last bits of her dreams close, daring to taste life.

Still she sings the songs of her ancestors, weaving gold from darkness.

She's desperate for a drink of light.

Magick falls from her eyes.

She sometimes can't tell what's a mirage and what is real.

Sometimes everything feels fake, and she can't tell if she is dreaming.

On these days, she's most dangerous to herself.

The voices are relentless.

diaries of a borderline iv

_____

She stares into pools of light, wondering if grace will find her before the monsters do.

She doesn't know what "I love you" means.

It sounds like saying goodbye.

Everyone she loves will one day die.

She knows this.

What will she do when the remnants of her family leave?

One day she'll be all alone, left to merely reminisce of the family she once called home.

She doesn't know what "I love you" means.

Love falls apart when the shadows with bloody fangs make love to her underneath her bed of razors.

She can't cut them out.

She's tried.

There's no escaping the devil once they learn your name.

Help me, she carves into her heart in the dark, hoping love is the spark to save her from dying.

Love never saved anyone—

she knows this.

The light was never for her, the monsters whisper.

She is legion.

She'll die if the light is too late.

Help . . .

diaries of a borderline v

_____

Sometimes she can't tell if she's dreaming.

She can see herself do things.

She gets lost in nightmares for daydreams.

The night seems awfully long when you can't close
your eyes to it.

Sometimes she can't tell if she's awake.

She picks at her skin, hoping the blood brings her back.

The blood brings her back.

The blood brings them back.

Sometimes she can feel she isn't here, but she doesn't know
where she is.

Time slows down.

Things become muted.

Sometimes it feels like she's falling into herself.

She lives whole moments outside of time, yet she knows, with
this life, she's only wasted days.

Sometimes she can't tell if she's better-off dead.

She misses them more than she let's on.

Grief is love trying to stand the test of time.

She doesn't know what "I love you" means.

She falls asleep to bloody prayers etched in her bedroom wall.

Save me.

diaries of a borderline vi

She's chronically in crisis.

She knows she has to live past the pain.

Suicide is an idol pulling her softly into a daydream.

The sirens call her back home with pills she'd only abuse.

She's chronically in crisis.

She doesn't know when she will heal the monsters.

She hopes forgiveness still brings her the happily ever after her heart wrote about in starry skies as the horizon told stories of the gods.

She wants to believe in her magick.

"Lumos" won't turn the lights on this time.

She's a Horcrux for her mother.

She hated her.

She knows this.

Love tried to absolve the curses her mother left with her.

The gallows swallow the light when the horizon devours the moon.

The constellations lead the devils to her.

She can't escape the cross.

They nail her wrist to pine.

Crown her with lies saying she's okay.

She's fine.

It's all in her mind.

She won't die this time.

She doesn't know if breath will ever want to fill her lungs again.

Each time she inhales, it feels like fire.

Reminding her she is the monster under her bed.

Her mother can't hurt her anymore, the therapists tell her.

Then why does her ghost possess her when the clock strikes thirteen and she can't seem to get the memories to quiet?

The past can be so loud.

She's chronically in crisis.

"Try this," the monsters demand.

"It'll stop the pain.

You won't feel anything anymore.

You believed me before.

Just trust me.

Take my hand.

Follow me into nothing.

We're all dead down here."

diaries of a borderline vii

_____

She still gets lost inside her head.

She's scared one day she won't find her way back.

How do we heal the wounds love leaves when it dies?

She still gets lost in her head, seduced by devils convincing her she's better-off dead.

"Did you hear what I said!"

Hope has grown cold.

She prays she dies before she gets old.

They say the good die young.

Bury her in sin and bone.

The princess dies at the end of this story.

Love doesn't bring the dead back.

The moonlight illuminates the date of her death is God's signature.

She still gets lost in her head, praying in tongues to tell the gods what her heart needs.

The devil always answers her prayers.

She's tired of being the only one who hates her.

She doesn't know sunflowers grow from tears.

She still gets lost inside her head.

It's midnight and she can't help but wonder if the stars will pronounce her dreams dead.

Bury them in moondust and fairy wings.

She doesn't believe magick is on the way anymore.

She's become a Horcrux for her mother.

Conjuring spells of worthlessness on her bedroom floor.

She still gets lost inside her head.

She still is lost to the dead.

diaries of a borderline viii

After her cities have burned at her fingertips,

she resurrects the monsters of ash and blood
to possess her being.

She surrenders her light.

Lucifer regains his halo.

After her dreams have fallen, she sighs as the voices have her.

The voices have her.

She can feel their hands pull her into her head.

She's already dead.

She plagues the living, hoping sunshine still wants her.

After her cities have burned and her hope decays,

the monsters become her.

The sun won't rise anymore.

The moonlight won't try to find her.

The stars won't lead her home this time.

After her cities burn at her fingertips,

she hopes they will remember her.

diaries of a borderline ix

———————

Her curse,

she falls apart every time she tries to put herself back together.

She'll never be whole.

She knows this.

It's etched in starlight still staining her bedroom window.

The monsters write on the walls.

She doesn't even remember why she started searching for herself in the beginning.

It's only given her more scars.

She's become her **BPD**.

She's special to the monsters with burning faces.

She's asked for help, hoping moon fairies fill her cracks with gold.

She gets nothing but traumatizing scars before she's old.

She'll never be the same again.

She wonders if she was ever whole or just always on the edge of sanity.

She hides it well.

A smile and pretty words get you far when you're a reflection.

She wishes she could be whoever the fuck she is.

At least she's special to the monsters with jagged teeth.

Her curse,

she falls apart before she can ever put herself back together.

diaries of a borderline x

She's lost in other realities, living the life she wishes she had.

This life isn't for her.

She knows this.

Love left when she lost them.

Anything goes.

She'll be burned at the stake for being something
man can't control.

She's lost in other realities, living the life she was supposed to.

This life is a nightmare breaking her spine.

She's a book she doesn't want to read anymore.

Sometimes life fills her bones with hope.

Then she's disappointed because where there is light,
there is always shadow. But where there is shadow,
not always is there light.

Hope requires faith, and she doesn't believe in silly fairy tales
anymore.

She's lost in daydreams, daring to taste the life she prays for.

Never again.

No closure comes from communing with the dead.

She doesn't know how to live.

Even time falls away from her.

She never knows what year she's in.

Can't you see it in her smile

the lies . . .

It's okay.

She's fine.

She's used their scorn.

Their "I love you" weighs her down with guilt.

She doesn't know what "I love you" means.

She's damned by the light.

She's lost in her head, imagining a life where Mother lived.

Where her sister survived.

What is she supposed to do now?

She keeps asking the stars staining the sky.

She never finds the answer.

She's tired of losing to her demons.

She is her mother's curse.

Does love really break curses?

diaries of a borderline xi

She's a creature of the void, walking the in-betweens, wishing life or death would decide where she can call home.

Everything has a home,

except her.

She's nostalgic for the light between the trees.

She swears she's from there.

Peace.

Hope.

Forgiveness.

But inside her mind, she connects the lines on her thighs to spell the date she didn't die.

Inside her mind, she's trapped in the in-between, wandering through purgatory scorned and demented, trying to fit into life when life has long since moved on.

She's stuck chasing memories that ruin her future.

She doesn't know how to live without them.

Death reaps the love it destroys.

Grief is the void it leaves.

She is a creature of the void, walking the in-betweens.

She prays she doesn't lose the fear and jump, but death is nothing compared to the monsters still left to face.

What do you do when life is the nightmare
you're trying to escape?

diaries of a borderline xii

_____

Her name means the punished one.

She can't escape the torture.

It's in her bones to hate herself.

She's never known anything else.

She learned it from watching love always disappoint her.

She learned it from being the most convenient thing for her mother to project her hate into.

She is her mother's curse.

They say we must be the ones to break our curses, but she's not sure she will ever find freedom in the stillness after rain.

Everything feels like trauma to her.

She can't tell the difference between "I'm busy"
and "I hate you."

She knows the difference, but it still hurts the same.

She is the second choice to herself.

Always busy trying to hide the fires burning her dreams up.

You can see the smoke in her eyes.

She's dying.

She smiles.

diaries of a borderline xiii

Her spirit goes away when the demons paint the walls red.

One look inside her mind and divinity is dead.

She can't find her halo.

She's blind to the light rotting in shadow. She'll die if the monsters find it.

Once the darkness takes, it never gives back.

Her spirit goes away when the demons demand their sacrifice.

A happy memory.

She overthinks until she ruins her peace and her life is a wake— they would only tell stories of how she was too sad to save.

She doesn't know where her spirit went.

She's forgotten the moonlight.

Dawn descends, and the velvety dark arrives to sacrifice the last parts of her she's learned to like.

She still calls the demons home.

The darkness of her family.

She still gets lost in dark caves, hiding the lies she's trying to escape.

They always find her underneath her bed.

She can't hide from them.

They taste her worthlessness.

She's a beacon for despair.

Without her spirit, she'll never be able to defeat the darkness.

diaries of a borderline xiv

To her, sadness and love are the same thing.

She's destined to be desperately lost in the dark.

The monsters steal her breath away.

Scars don't always heal.

Love doesn't bring the dead back, guilt does.

She's a necromancer how she bleeds over the Ouija,
conjuring ghosts with pretty eyes and dangerous smiles.

Her smile is riddled with maggots and lies.

She's the walking dead hoping the light brings her back.

She's lost in her head.

The monsters turn her heart into their heaven.

She's tortured daily.

She doesn't know what grace is.

She drowns in guilt.

Loneliness is her destiny.

It's written in her trauma.

She's sacrificed her hope to bargain with the monsters.

She can't win now.

diaries of a borderline xv

_____

"It's useless.

Don't do this."

She pleads with the devil, daring to rip hope from her ribs and name her just another sin.

She pleads with the devil to make her a demon.

She can be the sin _mortem_.

She'll die to keep the remnants of light beating in her chest.

She knows if the devil devours her dreams, she'll never find home.

She'd rather ruin all of it than fail.

She only has reasons to let go.

"It's useless.

Don't do this."

The demons call out behind the breeze warm with her blood.

"We can make you into what your mother wanted.

We can make your dreams come true.

Just surrender."

diaries of a borderline xvi

Sometimes she needs to remember,

and she can't.

Her sanity stops her from finding the pain in her veins.

Every day without them is the same.

Empty.

Lonely.

She's stuck in the past, petrified of her mother's lies that lead her into nothing.

Sometimes she needs to remember,

and it all feels fake.

Like she knows that's not her childhood, but she can't seem to remember it the way she wished it happened.

Still severed from her gifts—

it was the only way to protect them.

She's willing to let the monsters have them now.

She knows she can't save them anymore.

She's not worthy.

The hate riddled her bones with doubt.

She's the curse condemning her to heaven's gallows.

Sometimes when she needs to remember,

they flood her brain.

She sometimes remembers everything.

She sometimes can't stop thinking about it.

She sits at the edge of her bed, wondering if she'll press down again.

The blood brings her back.

She wishes something else would.

Everything feels like a dream when she's lost at sea.

The girl who falls out of time.

The girl who fell from love.

Sometimes she wonders if she will lead the monsters to moonlit coves illuminated by lantern bugs.

Her gifts lie here asleep.

She's tired of fighting shadows.

Maybe this is the only way to save herself.

diaries of a borderline xvii

If she had it her way,

she'd starve herself until the demons found her corpse useless.

She doesn't want to be here anymore.

None of her wishes have come true.

She doesn't know what to do with them.

Her dreams are dying.

She'll let them if it means the monsters won't ever have them.

She doesn't want to be her mother's curse.

She doesn't know how to set herself free.

If she had it her way, she would have never been born.

Life doesn't want her,

but it won't let her die.

She doesn't know how to hold her heart strong in the end.

When the monsters with knives for smiles hide behind her eyes.

She's a hurricane in disguise.

If she had it her way,

she would have left a letter a long time ago.

diaries of a borderline xviii

She can hear the sirens in the fog.

They sound like Mother.

She hated her too.

She didn't know what love was.

Now she doesn't know what "I love" means either.

Love feels like abandonment.

Love feels like being forced to hurt herself over and over and over just to feel wanted by the things she can't bury.

Love feels like falling apart at her fingertips.

She'll die when no one is watching.

She doesn't know why she even bothers anymore.

It's useless.

She's worthless.

Loveless.

Lonely.

Disappointed.

Life has long since murdered her joy with shots from a Glock to shock the rock she called herself.

She can't recognize that girl anymore.

The reflection of foggy waters pulls her under.

She'll drown on her own.

Why don't they know that?

The scars of winter freeze her brain in trauma.

One Christmas, she lost her mother.

Everything changed when she learned blood numbs the heart.

She wishes she never called the monsters family.

She can hear the sirens in the fog.

The sky is sunless.

The waves sound like rope.

The forests beyond these infested waters are still as graves.

There are bodies in the trees.

She can hear them cry out for her light.

She'll give it to them if she gives up.

She's tired, and life wasn't supposed to be her convincing herself she shouldn't drown.

Life never wanted her anyway.

She can't tell lies from truth anymore.

She can hear the sirens in the fog.

diaries of a borderline xix

She doesn't believe in anything except the devils writing
on her wrists.

She's learned to call it poetry.

She scribbles in blood.

She's dizzy.

She hasn't been eating.

She doesn't believe anything will save her anymore.

God is dead.

The devil ravages her mind.

She's chained by trauma.

Every time the light almost finds her, she turns away.

It burns when you aren't used to it.

There are no happily ever afters.

The princess hangs from her royalty.

She surrenders her divinity to the monsters
with knives for smiles.

She's shrouded in shadows now.

The voices got her.

The voices got her.

Hopelessness stalks her.

She's imprisoned inside her mind.

These ghosts possess her heart, hoping to rot her soul.

She's scared she doesn't know how to live without them.

The good die young.

And every day she's getting older.

She leaves letters behind in her poetry.

Her wrists tremble under the moonlight.

She's running out of time.

Bury her in cherry blossoms and twilight.

Her curse was being the only one who hated her.

Love never found her.

She fell out of sunshine.

What if her mother was right,

and she is the devil strangling the remnants of her light?

She is the monster under her bed.

Bury her in halos and gold.

She's better-off dead.

diaries of a borderline xx

Staring at the mirror with the lights off,

she hides her image in shadow.

She's scared to look into her eyes, to behold the little girl dying to remember what "I love you" means.

Dying to remember how to smile when she's alone.

Everything falls apart.

She knows she won't survive the winter.

The fear keeps her blood warm.

She's alive because she can't seem to die right.

She doesn't want to be here anymore.

She hides in the silhouette of stars scintillating through her window.

Her melanin glows in the moonlight.

She hates she survived.

Everything falls apart.

She's staring at the mirror with the lights off, wondering how she got this bad.

How she can't look at her reflection because she knows she will only see a waste wishing to be more than the voices tell her.

Her eyes hide meteor showers.

Magick is in her breath.

She's tired of protecting her gifts.

Let the monsters have them.

Staring at her reflection, she is losing the courage to turn the lights on.

diaries of a borderline xxi

_____

She hasn't known herself for quite some time now.

She's lost in a nightmare disguised as a daydream.

She's possessed by self-hate, trying to be anything but the sins staining her sleeves.

She cuts herself with shards of her halo, trying to force the light back in.

The stars condemn her as a monster.

She's the Horcrux of her mother.

Conjuring depravity through broken tongues till all she feels is nothing and everything.

She hasn't known herself for quite some time.

She wears masks, masquerading with the living, trying to pretend she belongs.

She's a mirror, so they believe her.

She doesn't know how to be herself.

The little girl hiding in the corner of her

soul still needs her to be the love she never got.

She doesn't know what "I love you" means.

She avoids the little girl trying to show her love is whatever makes the soul feel home.

She's homeless in a war zone, fighting to merely stay alive.

These demonic soldiers break hideous seals to open the terrors of her mind and force her to fall apart inside.

It sounds like her mom.

Mother always lies.

She hates her too.

Sometimes she curses herself, hoping to end the pain.

Bury her in diamonds and butterflies.

She's abandoned all hope.

She hasn't known herself for quite some time.

She died when they did.

Love doesn't bring anyone back to life.

In this story, Lazarus stays dead.

God was just another man.

Grace doesn't break the curse.

She'll die if the light doesn't reach her soon.

She's starting to become the voices.

diaries of a borderline xxii

It's harder to come back after the monsters take her.

She drifts off into a daydream.

The night seems like forever when the screams keep you awake.

She has learned when the voices are going to take her.

She can't stop it.

One moment she is there, then she isn't.

She's an empty grave, haunting her heart with memories
and reveries written in bone and blood, whispering,
"Remember me."

It's harder to come back when the monsters find her.

She wishes she wasn't this way.

She never thought things would turn out this way.

She can't help but escape to her bed of thorns.

They'll crucify her for being too depressed.

She's lost in her head, wondering when the light
will pronounce her dead.

Living a life she hates is the only thing she dreads.

She's not afraid of dying . . .

That's part of the problem.

It's harder to come back when the monsters abduct her.

They take her home.

She's scared she will always call the monsters family.

diaries of a borderline xxiii

She wears the stars on her sleeves.

She constellations scars on her wrists.

You can see the sorrow in her smile.

You can hear the dead when she laughs.

In this story, the monsters steal her joy away.

In this story, the devil possesses her heart.

She's drifted too far into the dark.

When you speak to the dead,

all of them can hear you.

The fox hears the rabbit and runs to it,

but not to help.

These monsters will devour her when she falls asleep.

They pick their teeth with her smile.

They drink her divinity in.

She'll die when no one is watching.

The little girl inside her chest still waits for her mommy
to come home.

She only wants to make her proud.

She only knows how to hate herself.

Her heart breaks every morning she wakes up.

She didn't think her life was going to be lived alone.

She used to believe love was enough.

"It's never enough,"
The monsters remind her.
They seduce her with pretty lies and moonshine.
She's drunk in regret.
The darkness devours the starlight.
She'll sign her dreams away if it means she can rest.
The devil regains his halo.
Still she knows hope is never lost—
the light always finds a way to weave gold from shadow.

diaries of a borderline xxiv

The feeling inside her chest has her wishing she was buried
alive in knives and scythes.

The reaper doesn't want her yet.

She hasn't suffered enough.

Her curse, to be drenched in sorrow.

Her bones soaked in worthlessness.

She's growing weaker every day.

Less hopeful.

She wonders if she'll ever find the safe haven her heart is
searching for.

They say she can be her own rescue, but she lured
the demons here.

She picked up the razor.

The lighter.

She stopped eating.

It's her fault the monsters love her.

She feeds them more than the fairies.

They'll reap her soul at moonrise.

She'll surrender the ghost if she can

become Beauty.

The beast devours Belle happily never after.

She doesn't want to die.

She can't see another way.

Where she breaks the curse of her mother.

What was done cannot always be undone.

She'll lead the monsters to the cove hiding pools of sunlight, trying to bloom moon roses in emerald and amethyst light.

She doesn't see another path than the one leading to bones and broken dreams.

It's okay.

She can rest this way.

The anguish of sunlight will always make her mourn.

The devil steals her halo.

diaries of a borderline xxv

She doesn't care about herself anymore.

Her hope has long since died.

She can't seem to end her life.

She's tried.

She wades in her tears, building a dam behind her eyes.

She'll drown when no one is watching.

This river is toxic.

Filled with disappointment,

self-hate,

grief,

and worthlessness.

She wishes she was the better everyone hopes for her.

She is the Mad Hatter lost in Neverland trying to believe in anything that will take her home.

Sadly, heaven doesn't hear her.

Only the devil answers her prayers.

She's grateful.

At least someone listens.

They mistake her smile and her ability,

as if she can do this by herself.

If she could,

she would've never picked up razor blades.

She would have never ripped the stars from her veins hoping the monsters would love her in the dark.

She's loved most by the dark.

She can't escape her symptoms.

She doesn't care about herself anymore.

Love doesn't wake the princess.

Let the dead be the dead.

She can't let them go.

She doesn't know why they think she can do it alone.

She knows she won't make it.

diaries of a borderline xxvi

_____

She hates the life she's created.

Everything was supposed to be different.

Her mom was supposed to love her,

her mom was supposed to live to see her blossom, her little sister wasn't supposed to die.

If anyone deserved death, it was her.

She'd prayed for it for years.

She just could never lose the strength to kill herself.

She tempts death with bated breath.

If only they would accept her final rose.

She could die happily ever after.

The lost girl fades into moonshine and fairy dust.

She hates the life she created.

She remembers being little, daydreaming at dusk of the life she would live, the dreams her heart would taste.

She's only wasted days.

Everything falls apart when the shadows murder the moonlight.

She can feel the serpents crawl between her thighs, corrupting her body with lies.

She tries to hide the signs by a smile that whimpers,
"It's okay, I'm fine."

She'll die if the light is too late.

diaries of a borderline xxvii

The light finally feels within reach.

She doesn't want it.

She's been possessed for so long, she's forgotten
what freedom feels like.

The light finally feels within reach,

but she can't let her mother go.

She loved her.

She doesn't know what "I love you" means.

But what if it means choosing to stay?

What if it is forgiveness that heals the monsters?

Compassion that holds the broken heart and laces it with gold
and fairy dust?

What if all along, she was the love she was looking for?

What if in this story, the lost girl saves herself?

The light finally feels within reach.

She's dying.

The remnants of starlight hidden in her

chest are fading.

She doesn't believe in her magick anymore.

Her mother hated her.

What is love but losing life to the dead?

She doesn't know what "I love you" means.

She can still hear the voices underneath the silence.

The light finally feels within reach.

What if hope is on the way?

diaries of a borderline xxviii

She's lost in-between the veil.

She doesn't know how to make the best choice for herself.

She's always chosen wrong.

The voices pull her heartstrings.

She's a puppet for her demons.

When she can't, they can.

She believes in them more than the happily ever afters knocking on her door.

She's learned not to trust the light.

In it, she burns like a witch.

Magick doesn't cool the fire.

She is legion.

She conjures her mother's devils at twilight, hoping she feels anything but loneliness pulling her further into her coffin.

She's terrified of dying.

She's convinced life isn't for her.

She's better-off dead.

Bury her in lost love and grief.

She doesn't know what "I love you" means.

"I love you" is a curse scarring her body with hate.

She wishes she didn't hate herself anymore.

She wishes her mother loved her.

She wishes her mother knew what love was.

She wishes she had died instead of her.

She has been asking for death since she fell out of the light.

She's lost in-between the veil.

The monsters steal her hope.

She's tired of the ambivalence.

It doesn't matter if she lives or dies.

The monsters will have her light regardless.

The devil will regain his halo at the witching hour.

Three a.m. prayers don't make it to heaven.

There is no god willing to save her.

Only the devil rests on her shoulders.

She's lost in-between the veil.

She can feel the borderline in her chest starving for her divinity.

If she surrenders now, she'll die.

She's terrified of dying.

diaries of a borderline xxix

She's scared.

Her mother broke her.

She's terrified.

The monsters put her back together.

She doesn't know what happiness is.

Everything feels like trauma.

The light inside her is shattered.

Her mind is a haunted asylum of ghosts.

She knows the memories demand to be relived.

They wrap every happy situation into what if they leave.

What if they die?

What if they abandon her when she needs them most?

That's how it went in the past.

Her mother.

Her sister.

Nothing she ever loved survived.

If only she loved herself enough to want to

stay.

She's guilty.

Her crime,

not saying it back.

Sometimes she thinks about cutting her tongue out so she can never say those words again.

She doesn't know why "I love you" is an empty graveyard.

She's scared she'll only fall apart more when the rest of her love dies.

What the fuck will she do then?

diaries of a borderline xxx

_____

She never imagined she'd live past fourteen.

Fifteen.

Eighteen.

Twenty-one.

She was certain she'd kill herself by twenty-five.

She's turning twenty-nine now.

Her life feels like a dream she's lost in.

She doesn't know how to grow the light blooming
inside her chest.

She doesn't know what "I love you" means.

She doesn't know what to do with the wishes
that never came true.

She's afraid she'll murder the dreams trying to bloom
from her fingertips.

She still hates the stardust coursing through her blood.

She doesn't know how to not feel hopeless.

Worthless.

Loveless.

Light is finally on the way.

She can feel it warm her bones.

She's confused.

The voices still call her out from lonely shadows.

The monsters still visit her at sunrise and sunset.

Yet something inside her fell into place when she started to believe in her divinity.

She doesn't know what to do if she lets the devils go.

She doesn't know who she'll be if she heals the monsters.

A soft whisper underneath the breeze calls her home.

What if time is healing her as we speak?

For the first time, she stands a chance against the darkness.

She's terrified of letting her mother go.

She knows she has to.

diaries of a borderline xxxi

It is what she names herself in the dead of night that binds her
to the lies in her wrist and her thighs,

to find a reason to let go of the remnants of her light.

She's dying to fight, but the monsters have stolen her courage.

She's hopelessly hoping she still stands a chance against the dark.

diaries of a borderline xxxii

She's trying to let go of the guilt.

The shame.

The fear.

She's trying to rescue her heart from the dark.

She's lost in-between suicide and happily ever after.

She has always chosen wrong.

History shows she's more broken than she admits.

Her mother hated her.

She's confused.

The dissonance breaks her bones.

She's paralyzed by her past.

Abuse haunts her joy.

She can't feel the light without bleeding.

She doesn't know what "I love you" means.

She's trying to let go of her monsters.

Heal the parts of her still lost to the abyss.

Still, she stares in the mirror, trying to find the little girl

behind her smile who used to laugh, carefree.

Still, she hates the treasure beating in her chest.

She doesn't know if she'll survive the war.

The sirens chant underneath the shadows.

She'll die if the light reaches her too late.

prophecies of a borderline i

She stopped cutting herself to feel love.

She stopped abandoning the little girl crying behind her smile.

She stopped hating who she was.

She stopped living for her dead mother.

Finally, she learned to see the diamonds glistening behind her eyes.

She was what the stars are made of.

Resilience.

They generate their own warmth.

Their own light.

Even in a sea of darkness, they shine through.

She became a constellation.

Guiding the monsters home.

Finally, the curse is broken.

Her soul's light is drenched in divinity.

The past is behind her.

The darkness couldn't get her anymore.

prophecies of a borderline ii

She only knows what abandonment feels like.

Love leaves her just when she needs it most.

She's afraid if she loves again, they will die.

That love won't be enough to save anyone,

not even herself.

So she burns love to the ground and poisons the land where love once bloomed.

She's unworthy.

A devil's harlot.

What would want to love her enough to stay?

Her own mother died loving her.

She loved her dying little sister.

She always wished life loved her enough to let her go too.

She never thought she'd love life.

She never believed happily ever after would pirouette across the ballroom floor of her soul and remind her tomorrow is what we live for.

That with the sun mercy comes.

Grace finds its way to us through breaking dawn.

She never believed life would teach her the lessons she had been killing herself to learn.

What the fuck does she do now?

No one ever told her what to do when the monsters regain their halos, when hell's fire finally subsides, and her soul tastes the first drop of light from eternity's river.

What do we do when our wishes come true?

Does she deserve to love life without them?

What if she has finally outgrown the demon slicing her smile with knives because sorrow once turned her heart to stone?

But light comforts the soul.

She only knows what self-hate feels like.

The way it slithers up her spine and decimates the garden growing in her chest.

She learned she would get the love she yearned for if she always fell apart.

She's lost most of her pieces to the darkness, but still starlight wraps itself around her when the night is cruel.

She finds home in the constellations cascading across the velvety night, reminding her she is on the path to healing the wounds left by the hearts who didn't know how to love her.

Who weren't ready to love her.

Who lied and manipulated her heart into thinking her soul wasn't deserving of the love sunshine brings.

She's learning healing the monsters means forgiving herself for ever choosing them over herself.

She buries her nightmares in the earth, knowing Mother Nature turns all things beautiful.

To the wind, she leaves the wishes she's grateful
never came true.

In the waters, she remembers she is who will save her heart from the perilous ghost haunting her present.

In the fire, she cleanses her divinity.

She still gets lost in the dark forest home to wolves foaming at the mouth for her spirit.

She still stands at the edge of her soul and wonders if she will ever have the courage to fly.

She's learning the key to healing her abandonment is not neglecting her heart when it speaks.

She's learning the key to self-love is doing more of what makes us feel safe,

seen,

and treasured.

She's learning she was never the monster her mother named her.

The hexed princess dies for herself, and from her ashes a goddess is born.

Part II

This Is Why
She Falls Apart

she finally falls apart

_____

She still sends wishes to her mother's graveyard, hoping to bloom beauty from grief.

The moonlight heals her scars.

The twilight breaks her silence.

Tears are simply wishes that have died.

She tears herself apart trying not to die.

Dying is easy.

Choosing to live is hell.

They say heaven is in the home we make for ourselves.

Her heart is a prison she cannot escape.

She still weeps dreams at her mother's headstone, hoping to find the parts of herself her mother took.

hope chooses to live

_____

She hears the songs beyond the trees,

telling her heaven is found only after we crawl through our hell.

There we will taste pools of light sweeter than love and cream.

She can feel the light warm her skin on the days her heart is most open.

Dreams breathe her full again, once she chooses to leave the graveyard, still depriving her of herself.

She'll die if she dances with the devil.

There's no escaping the monster under her bed filling her head with dread.

She hates what it says.

She's always been better-off dead.

"Hold on to me," she pleads in her sleep.

The song beyond the trees guides dawn's light, knowing love is never late.

what does 'I love you' mean

Sometimes she can't remember herself before the abuse.

Before the hatred her mother taught her.

Before the hopeless nights wondering why her last words were "I love you."

She doesn't know what "I love you" means.

It feels like self-harm.

It tastes like disappointment.

It looks like never being good enough to earn her love.

She can't love herself either.

These days, she struggles to eat.

She's quieter.

Lost in her head, wishing she was dead.

She's seventeen again, standing over her mother's grave, wondering how she is supposed to feel with the monsters her mother left behind.

possessed

_____

She misses her little sister.

They were supposed to taste life's dreams together.

She's her loneliest at nightfall.

Everything falls apart when her mother's ghost haunts her hope.

She's scared of the light.

She's scared of having to face joy alone.

How can she be happy without Allie?

She was supposed to be an architect.

She loved drawing.

She was an artist.

Compassionate.

Patient.

All the things I am not, she thinks to herself, pouring a bottle of pills down the sink.

She's fine with the demons lurking in the broken parts of her.

satin and wildflowers

Sometimes she prays she dies young.

A life fully lived still feels like moments passed.

She wishes she had told her mother how she felt then, when she was passing.

Why burden the dying?

In her dreams, she has to save her little sister or her sister.

She can never choose.

Identity or possibility.

She kills herself in her dreams, hoping that in death, happily ever after is found.

She wakes up lost.

a good day

She stands by the river.

Its ebb and flow echoes in her bones.

Lightning sparks behind her eyes.

She is strong enough to defeat the monsters with knives for smiles harvesting her sunshine.

Her curse is she is the only one who believes
they will defeat her.

They will kill her if they can.

When will she fight back with thunder in her voice?

She stands by the river.

Today, she will survive.

She goes home.

Warms a bath.

She loves the tears away.

Her heart is still broken.

This is how she begins to sew her dreams back together.

plagued

_____

She spends her time lost in nightmares.

She's always soothing her mind.

Distracting, hoping to spend a little more time in the light
before the light starts to feel like trauma.

She's forgotten her happiest memories.

Her life was watching her fear-filled mother die
wanting to love her.

She spends her time awake in a dream, crucifying the child
inside her for not knowing what to say.

Sometimes she remembers there was nothing she could say.

Why burden the dying?

12:00 a.m.

_____

When she dissociates, she goes to places her soul fears most.

She hangs from the promises never made between mother and daughter.

She died too that day.

She finds her way back to the present.

The light phases through her soul.

She's lonely.

She's loved her lost ones longer than she's known them.

Who will remember them when she's the last one in her family?

Who will love them if she can't?

What if loving her lost mother is too heavy for her now?

What if she was right?

She finds her way back to the present.

It's time for bed.

scarlet letter

———————

Not a day passes when the torment doesn't end.

She's a ghost haunting herself.

Watching herself abandon her heart over and over, hoping all mothers love their children.

She hated her.

At least, that's what she showed.

Her birthdays were the only times she wasn't walking on eggshells trying to appease and please the mother of monsters marking her.

She is the mark of the beast trying to find her halo amid persimmons and parables, pretending she's worth anything more than the disappointment wasting her days.

She's the hexed princess.

Wasting fairy tales found in heaven's bosom where the sun sleeps.

She'll destroy herself hoping the torment ends for good.

good days i

Some days she remembers how to smile.

How to laugh without worry.

Some days she knows how to bask in sunbeams calling her heart from shadows and ash.

Some days light is the love she feels when hope has found her.

She relearns how to love herself.

This time,

she knows life is on her side.

baltering through sunlight

Sometimes she can feel the warmth in-between the breeze.

Light lends her heart a hand in letting the roses wilt at her mother's graveyard.

Let the dead be the dead, she tells herself on the better days, when she can remember who she is.

Still she believes the monsters at 3:00 a.m. scarring her skin with lies.

Sometimes dawn pirouettes across waking horizons into her bedroom, pouring into her heart's cracks.

Hope still mends the broken.

Sometimes she is the light between the trees, calling the other parts of her forgotten to shadow home.

adopted

Ruby wrists shatter against the black of night.

"Help me."

Crying out to whatever god or devil is willing to answer
her prayers.

She'll surrender her grace to the one who ends her torment.

The devil always collects.

She can feel the fires.

She opens her eyes.

The rain scratches against her window.

"It was just a dream."

She carves a smile into her face.

She's a lost girl wading in rivers of grief.

The razor has always been her second mother.

scarred starlight

She strangles herself with her halo.

Nothing feels good without them.

The divinity that was supposed to save her is the reason she's giving up.

Everyone else thinks she's a light leading the lost home,

when she can't even save herself from nightfall.

This is why she falls apart.

Hiding behind the screams she's scared to let out.

What if she let the monsters consume her grace?

Would she finally show up for herself in death?

good days ii

_____

She is grateful for the moments she's most present.

Plagued by nightmares.

Lost in daydreams.

It is when she remembers who she is that the light is able to kiss the seeds of hope starting to blossom from her chest.

On these days she is a safe haven for the little girl still crying in her mother's graveyard.

She is grateful for a moment,

she shows up for herself.

a lost girl

_____

When the monsters arrive with knives for smiles, reaping the dreams left behind from scarred stars,

she clicks her heels together, hoping broken moonbeams lead her home.

voodoo

_____

Self-hate is a ritual she knows too well.

She can trace the lines on her wrist and her thighs, screaming, hoping the light recognizes she's never been fine.

She hides in her mind.

The monsters conjure themselves awake to take her light and murder it with a stake.

She's nothing but a waste.

She sacrifices her grace to her mother, wondering if Lazarus still rises.

When you speak to the dead,

all of them hear you.

fairy tales

_____

She still stands under wilted branches casting cherry blossoms to rotted earth.

Self-hate was sewn into her heart.

She doesn't know how loving herself is supposed to feel.

Bury her in cherry blossoms and sorrow.

She holds hope in cut palms, trying to peek through the veil to see her future.

Chaos always comes with a price.

She stands still under bleeding branches forsaking prayers made to silky slivers of silver dripping between the trees.

She is learning to weave compassion out of learned self-hatred.

What if she learns to love herself for the times she's survived?

What if she learns lost love transmutes to light to warm us when winter's dark blankets our spirit?

What if none of it was her fault?

hopeless ever after

_____

Maybe she is the light she's hoping rescues her
from her mother.

The little girl inside is still petrified, crying, hoping love can
save her mommy from dying.

It can't.

It couldn't.

She knows this all too well.

Love never saved anything.

dying

_____

She wishes missing her mother didn't cost her dreams.

prophecies

Loneliness tells her it's better to be dead and missed than be alive and abandoned.

She knows she's loved through the difficult days.

She's scared.

She doesn't know how to hold on to the light's love.

She destroys everything precious to her.

Until she's lonely once again.

coming home

_____

Written on her wrist are stories of how she survived every monster slithering in the graveyard of her mind where her mother went to die.

Written in her smile is a strength that could reach the stars in one bound.

Her heart was forged from starlight, kissed by sunshine, breathed full by hope.

She is immaculate in her imperfections.

Yet she bleeds the dreams that will save her,

never knowing she's her savior.

good days iii

Eventually, she will see there was nothing in the light to fear.

The light can be found in sunshine and moonbeams.

First light and starlight.

Sooner than later, she will come to love and accept her gift is in how she feels.

How loving herself back together is how she plants her wishes into pale-blue skies to hold her when she needs love most.

She creates the hope that will save her when shadows return.

Grace remembers her name.

It is written in how moonlight heals her scars.

How sunshine catches her tears.

Eventually, she will see it was never her that was broken.

starved

_____

She tends to her mother's graveyard more than
her own garden.

She doesn't know how to love herself without punishment.

Look at how she treats her body!

She learned this from her.

To her, dying and self-love feel like the same thing.

She was eight when her mother first cursed her.

Fourteen when her mother left her haunted.

Seventeen when her mother's ghost broke her for good.

Bury her with warm hugs at twilight by the riverbed
where the fay glow.

She was always going to die when she found her happily
ever after.

grieving roses

Dearest little sister,

I still think about you at last light when the skies are
our favorite colors.

I still wish I could tell you everything is working out for my
good and still I'd rather have you here.

I don't know what I'm supposed to be if not your big sister.

I loved you most.

forgiveness

_____

Still, the rooster crows the sun awake at dawn.

The monsters recede back into the hallowed hallways of her broken heart.

She's loneliest when they leave.

She's called them family for as long as she can remember.

It's no wonder she conjures them during the day.

She doesn't know who she is unless she's falling apart.

Still, she wakes with the sun, hoping to love herself a little more than the day before.

you

_____

Dear self,
she begins to write.

I'm sorry Mommy neglected you.
I'm sorry Mommy ruined your hope.
I'm sorry Mommy hurt your heart.

I'm sorry you still treat us like she did.
You're learning to be the better I deserved then.

Sincerely,
You

a reaper's wish

_____

One day she knew she would die,

staring a scythe in the face with both joy and fear.

Time erodes mountains to meal while kings lose crowns to
graveyards of wishes that have passed.

One day she knew the devil would dare to call her back to rule
a land where rainbows rot to disappointment.

If one thing is certain,

nothing escapes life alive.

Sometimes she thinks she's ready to die,

but then there are moments when home feels a lot like standing
in ponds filled with dreams,

ready to resurrect the parts of her dead from grief.

Moments when everything comes together and tears are
replaced with a smile from the way sunshine calls her back to
the home she thought was lost to trauma.

This is why she falls apart.

Home doesn't feel like home forever.

She hasn't felt home since love died loving her.

Part III

Leaving Her
Mother's Graveyard

abandon all hope

_____

In this graveyard where bones crumble to the touch
of cold winds,

she lies in a coffin of misery and fear.

She's miserable, living a life without the ones she had hoped
would love her full.

She's terrified.

She knows she doesn't want to spend the rest of her days sad,
but she's scared to prove her mother wrong.

She'll die in the same grave if she doesn't decide to rise with
dawn, trying to lead her broken heart to the pieces she knows
will restore her.

She knows every place in this cemetery of trauma, binding
these memories to her wrist with nails,

she's the Worthless Christ.

Crucified for her mother's transgressions against her.

She'll die in this grave of alcohol and painkillers to numb the
roaches crawling up her thigh to make a home in the womb
where her dreams once were.

Starving vultures fly over her hopeless temple hoping they too
will enjoy her with the monsters.

Everything dies eventually.

Yet, every time she's tried, she's survived, questioning still if her mother was right and she was better-off a memory.

The more she thinks the more she remembers how monsters and mothers feel like the same thing.

How punishment is just another way to say, "I love you."

She still loves herself wrong under a starless scarlet sky.

Sometimes she knows this can't be home forever.

There is a piece of her heart holding on to the last dream keeping her tethered to light.

Sometimes, she knows she's outgrown the grave of her mother.

Sometimes, forgiveness wipes her tears with love as the sunlight peeks through scarlet skies, scattering the starving vultures hungry for her corpse.

Sometimes, she knows life is for her.

Still, on restless nights, she finds comfort in the lies of her mother.

She's scared to let her mother go.

She'll die if she doesn't?

fading souls

_____

In her dreams she leaves.

A land of reveries awaits her tired eyes.

Love greets her in a forest of cherry blossoms still budding over a river reflecting the magick hour.

"Believe in the magick your soul is made of.

It will guide you back here, to your home.

The place you know calls from the stars yearning to see you bloom.

Believe in the future your heart paints across azure skies full of cotton shapes telling stories of a little girl who finally leaves her mother's grave.

Stories of a little girl who finally embraces her gifts to heal her hurts and bloom beautifully as her spirit always intended.

Hope is in the future your heart wishes."

She opens her eyes.

A tear falls from her earthy cheeks.

She can't feel her legs.

She's been nailed to this casket since she was a child.

How does she walk when her bones are broken?

She is malnourished.

The sunlight blinds her eyes.

Her mother's ghost haunts her.

She won't let her escape!

"Don't you love me?"

"If you forget me, I'll have no one."

"If you leave, who will remember me?"

"I don't want to be forgotten."

"I know," she says, closing her eyes to the sunlight fading off her skin.

Each time she surrenders, her dream dies a little more.

what if there's more to life than punishment

Days pass as she wastes away, wondering when she will muster up
the courage to save herself.

The vultures reappear overhead, cawing in cracked skies for her
heart's corpse.

She sits, hoping to wake up and find the strength to rise with
the dawn and cast mother's monsters away.

She knows there is a land for her.

One of halos and golden roses shimmering in a lilac-blue sky,
revealing the secrets she thought were lost to abuse.

They say that her gifts will save her from the monsters.

To her, she's useless to herself.

Hopeless in her ability to rescue herself.

What gifts could she possibly have to save her from
this graveyard?

it starts with hope

She dreams of meadows of periwinkle and sunflowers swaying in the warm breeze.

The doves chirp as the swallows sing peace, for the lost daughter has found her way back to herself.

There is a ball of light floating in the middle of a pond of nimbus clouds.

She walks toward the ball of light, feeling its pull as if she'd known it her whole life.

The closer she gets, nature falls quiet.

The doves watch with anticipation.

The swallows smile.

With dying hands she reaches out to touch the floating light calling her name from beyond the grave.

She falls through the clouds.

She wakes up in this casket of roaches and razor blades and stands for the first time.

She is in a hole of memories years deep.

Abuse tried to break her.

It almost did.

But for the first time,

she feels her mother was wrong.

The ground trembled.

The scarlet cracked sky dissipated to blue.

She drank in the sunlight.

She had been starving herself of the very things that would heal the parts of her she needs to survive the monsters trying to still bind her in her mother's name.

As above,

So below.

leaving the grave behind

From inside the casket, she watched as the elm tree bloomed and withered as spring fell to winter.

She realized everything passes with enough time.

In passing, new things sprout life and life basks in the certainty our dreams outweigh our hurts.

She stood tall and climbed from the grave.

The vultures cawed as the voices from scarlet skies berated her.

"You're worthless."

"Who says you don't have to suffer?"

"Don't you want to remember her?"

"You're supposed to suffer."

"The punished one."

"You're wrong,"

she finds the bravery to voice as the sunlight starts to reach her skin.

She drinks in hope like a waterfall of light comforting the parts of her desperate to heal.

The vultures antagonize her, hoping she'll give in like she used to.

"She hated you."

"Look at what you've done to yourself because of her."

She was scared to die.

I was punished for living.

I am learning how to let the dead go.

Scarlet skies absolved to lilac blue.

The vultures scattered at the authority she found.

She stood for the first time underneath the elm tree.

Fireflies fluttered in dusk light.

She sighed.

She could taste redemption in the breeze.

Surely, the monsters would be back.

The darkness doesn't give up without a fight.

It takes as much as it can, always wanting more.

She had nothing left to give.

first steps

She stares at the casket.

The stained razors alter her reflection.

From outside the grave, she is nothing like her mother.

From outside the grave, she can untangle the lies her mind finds to convince her she's better-off leaving her heart behind.

She used to see herself as worthless.

Broken.

The lost ghost left behind by her mother.

The grave calls to the broken parts of her yet to be healed,

reminding her life is easier if you sleep it away.

"It's okay to be left behind.

You'll be closer to Mom that way."

No.

She clenches her fist and walks toward the bright bolts of blue trying to lead her to the home she knows is for her.

a future worth fighting for

Even after the dust clears,

the bones become soil.

Soil homes seeds to sprout roots of safety so that other gifts
can blossom.

What will she grow here?

Now that everything is falling into place for the first time?

She once believed she was nothing.

She's learning she can be everything.

She'll heal her soul to mend her heart, even if it kills her.

But it won't.

She's been tested by shadows and fire.

Blood is no foreign foe.

She will face the darkness with tears in her eyes.

Bittersweet.

She loved the monsters once.

Now, she loves herself more.

It was time to hold infinity in her hands and weave the tapestry
telling her tale to be one she would love and never forget.

One of hope.

Where holidays didn't remind her of funerals anymore.

Where she would come home to a family after a long day of work and be reminded by every smile and warm hug why she chose to stay all those years ago.

How she learned to accept the love light leads us to

How she became a home for herself first.

Part IV

The Gifts
She Found

the gifts she finds

Dear little one,
she writes.

Where have you gone?

Why do you hide from me?

I'm sorry I treated you like her.

I wouldn't trust me with my heart either.

I can't even remember the promise we would make when the demons found us.

I can't even remember what my heart longed to keep safe all those years ago.

I'm sorry I abandoned you each time you cried for my attention.

I'm sorry I'm still torn between loving you and pleasing Mother.

Pleasing Mother hurts.

When will I learn self-harm and growth don't have to feel like the same thing?

Sincerely,

The me healing in mountain skies of fuchsia and apricot

gifts waiting to be found

A soft, childlike whisper asked from behind violet butterflies,

"You aren't one of the monsters, are you?"
She peeked amber-brown eyes from out fluttering wings.
"No," the hopeless girl replied, unsure.
She didn't want to be one of the monsters, but what else
could she be?

"I don't believe you. You feel like the monsters.

"I don't believe you. They all say they're my friends, then
they hurt me. What if you're like them?" the childlike voice
pondered.

"A part of me wants to believe you," the little voice giggled.

"Will you help me find what I lost? If so, I'll believe you."

"What is it?" the hopeless one questioned.

"You'll know when you find it,"
She giggled.

The hopeless one was alone in herself again.

What was she to search for?
How would she know when she found it?

Part V

The Gifts of Water: The Heart Is How We See Ourselves

the gifts of water

She formed a covenant with a vow said to the spirit
of the water.

Teach me to wade in tempestuous tides of the heart.

Teach me to walk on the reflection of moonlight across pools
of indigo.

Guide me deep into the mystery of me, and urge me to uncover
my soul's secrets.

Teach me how to wade in wishes waiting to come true.

As above,

so below.

falling into herself

The waters of the sky reflecting iterations of time show her the past, present, and future.

She peeks into the cloudy past.

She only remembers being hurt.

She's hoping her history holds a love their heart protected from the monsters Mother left behind.

The stars twinkle in the ripples of pools of time, illuminating moments of love in constellations.

Surely, she would find what she lost.

soul diving

She wades in rivers of divinity draping the stars across
starlit cheeks.

Pools of hope rejuvenate her tired spirit.

The graveyard still whispers nothings into her heart, hoping
she'll open the door to let the monsters in.

With hindsight, she remembers what they did to her.

How they made her feel.

What they made her to do herself.

She'd be dead if it wasn't for the love she learned
how to give herself.

She wades in ponds of serenity reflecting in ripples of
prophecies yet to pass.

She's learning how to feel into the parts of her still holding on
to Mother's hand.

Water remembers.

She'll never forget.

In order to dive deeper into her dreams, she will have to leave
the past behind.

She's made it this far.

How grateful her heart is, knowing she chose to hold on.

Starlight glows brightest when darkness falls.

She etches her name into time, knowing the gift of life is in how deep the heart can feel.

How much love the heart can hold.

How hope heals its scars with forgiveness's kiss.

How the sunlight can begin to warm memories sorrow once filled.

tending to ourselves

She used to believe the sky was sad when it rained.

She used to believe she would have always drowned herself in the shadows of her mother's ghost.

She used to believe, in order to be loved, she must water herself down.

She was always too much while never being enough at all.

She learned to walk on the water, stare into its folds, and manifest her future.

She used to believe everyone else deserved to heal except her.

How wrong she was.

How thankful she is now that she feels how warm her love is.

closer to the sun

———————————

Forever fills her lungs with purpose.

Art falls from her cheeks.

Healing showers her with renewal.

She bathes in the love she once denied herself.

How good it feels to lift her eyes to infinity.

She can see her reflection in the watery sky.

How different she looks as she learns to see herself with love.

Whispers still find her.

There is still a battle, for the past doesn't let us go as easily as we wished.

The scars on her wrists and thighs still hide from the light when she smiles.

She doesn't know how to love the parts of her that had to learn how to survive without a mommy,

but she's learning.

untitled I

_____

Betrayed by her mother,

she learned how to betray her heart when the skies were young.

It's all she can remember.

It's all she's able to feel when she tries to love herself.

She's betraying herself to feel her mother's love.

Self-love still feels like self-harm sometimes, when the monsters mutilate the night with dissociated nightmares in which she's trapped, reliving the moments that broke her hope.

She's hopelessly lost in-between this animosity and dissonance.

She doesn't trust her intuition.

She's always abandoned herself for her mother.

She's learning that showing up for herself is choosing the things reminding her to love herself anyway.

Water doesn't judge the form it takes,

but when it can run free,

it always, always chooses to be boundless.

a wish she's making

Rainbow rivers meet at the pond of dreams.

This pond has no bottom and is filled with courage and mysticism.

She's realizing the way to her dreams was always going to be diving into her heart's depths to baptize herself in the well of her soul.

Her magick was always her choice.

Rainbow rivers ripple across time's essence.

Dreams come true when we need them to most.

revelations

_____

At the edge of nothing, lies everything.

In the heart of suffering, hope is born.

Time pauses when love blooms.

Time aches when love dies.

Still at the edge of nothing, she is everything she needs to be at this time to bloom the love leading her out from depraved graves of ghosts haunting her heart's haven.

Monsters dissolve in forgiveness.

It was how she shifted her eyes to see the gifts in the oceans storming behind her gaze.

Skylight drips into her.

She can hear the rivers of old stories ignite her bones.

She's beginning to remember.

untitled ii

_____

Flashbacks find their way into the ripples of her mind, echoing traumas she long since thought she'd forgotten.

For her own good.

But the mind always remembers when it is ready.

Thoughts flood her brain, muddying her heart's rivers.

She breathes in starlight.

She remembers how to cast the light to absolve the shadows stealing her joy.

She remembers the scared moments, standing in ponds of dreams, daring to become real for her soul to savor.

She would face her fears with the sword of the covenant between her and the little one behind her eyes wondering with bated breath what this once hopeless one will do next.

One violet butterfly appears to guide her. From out of the shadows, she hears a distant giggle.

Part VI

The Gifts of Earth: A Soul Sprouts

tears still bloom beautiful things

Trauma is what turns the seeds yearning to bloom into the soul's dreams afraid to come true.

Nurture and nature are how the self is formed.

What if nurture felt like a second choice and that disfigured her nature?

She used to only believe in the power of a razor.

Save her!

The ground shakes as a seed nurtured with water blooms tender anemones.

A hummingbird perches upon the newly bloomed beauty beautifully.

Cascading leaves blow in-between the morning dew.

Hope leads the heart to new pieces of itself, the soul simply asks us, "Will we stay long enough to find them?"

untitled iii

Seven tapestries of light braid the sunset together.

The earth holds the warmth in her soil.

The earth knows to save what keeps it alive.

The soul is this way too.

Hoping the heart holds on to the magick driving budding petals of dreams to flourish into meadows of fairy tales come true.

In darkness, the seed grows, bathing silently in light and rain.

It takes its first breath above ground, hoping its home will tend it to beauty.

Everything deserves to have the chance to bloom.

the first mother

A letter from the first mother, Nature.

Dearest loved one,

I know how lonely being can feel when the light fades and we forget life's gift is in the present.

Being present is to remain open so you can make the best choice.

I hope you learn to choose yourself, as I have learned to choose what blooms me.

When I was young, I felt sorry when my winters would freeze the meadows of sunflowers trying to warm themselves
back to life.

When my fear quaked the ground and caused mountains to split and oceans to rise.

When I would cry for weeks and flood the very life
I hoped to sustain.

As I grew wiser with experience and curiosity, I realized the sunflowers unthaw under spring's kiss.

The mountains that split form new homes for life finding their way out from winter's cold.

Seeds carried by flooded rivers birth new miracles in lands where maybe miracles would never bloom.

With life comes pain.

And the thing about pain—

it demands to be felt.

Onward was always going to be the way to the home you deserved then and the home you dream of now.

Find peace in the trees towering overhead. They look to the north, receiving guidance from the mountains.

Find serenity in the rivers rushing down to grow the love that sustains life.

Find hope in the way the wind holds the birds.

Your spirit wishes to hold you this way,

tender and secure.

Trusting the souls process is how you reconnect with nature.

I am rooting for you.

untitled iv

They say the one who breaks the glass judges how shattered its reflection becomes.

"Why do we reject the parts of us trying to thrive!" she screamed.

The earth hummed.

The air stilled.

The water waited.

The skies turned red, and crackling whispers oozed from out the holes in scarlet black.

This was a part of you, my dearest.

Healing and blossoming and thriving means acknowledging the past you survived did happen, but it is not all that is happening, nor is it all that will happen.

As I grew full in years, I learned healing was a constant renewing of vows to self-forgiveness, self-acceptance, and self-love.

I learned to love myself even when hurricanes decimated dreams built from the ground up, holding hope and love in-between four walls.

I learned to love myself when the sparrow sang in the yew tree just before twilight fell, as the night awoke.

I love myself no more or less, whether it be a hurricane or a meadow with clear skies or air that smells like cotton candy.

I learned as pain turned to lessons, and lessons taught me when to blossom and when to enjoy the view right in front of me.

The girl breathed as the sky grounded itself back to shades of promises kept.

She looks at the violet butterfly fluttering above her right shoulder.

She's grateful she left her mother's graveyard.

She's never felt whatever this feeling was.

Safety.

Her bones sighed in relief.

Finally,

she'd started creating a place for her to stay.

A place in herself to call home.

untitled v

If one flower can bloom beautifully,
maybe others can too.

divinity blossoms from light weaved from shadows

_____

She buried the bones of her mother deep in the womb
of the earth.

Memories dropped her to her knees.

Her hands started to shake.

The sky flickered like C-4.

A whisper fell into her ears,

"Your mother was the devil's whore.

If you abandon her, she'll never love you anymore.

Don't you want to be a good daughter?"

She laughed.

"Is that your best?"

She breathed in violet light that smelled like honeycomb
and vanilla.

The monsters will always try to steal the joy right from
underneath our smiles.

Strength comes in the bravery to choose keeping what we hope
is more sacred than the shadows watching from the grave.

The sky bloomed lilies and nightingale.

The fireflies spelled out a name in cursive lightning, lighting the anemones blossoming beautifully.

She is grateful to feel the heart she feels safe in most is beginning to be her own.

the way was always in

Digging in soul's soil, she's looking for the key she left behind.

It was supposed to remind her of something treasured.

Kept.

Sacred.

The earth keeps our secrets silent.

She judges nothing felt by the heart or spoken by the soul.

As she digs into her soul, she finds her mind's pollution trying to rot her heart's meadow from the inside.

The voices smile.

She breathes in trust.

The violet butterfly hums in her ear.

"Dig deeper.

The pain won't stop us anymore."

she's starting to answer her own prayers

As she dug, the voices tried to tempt her to stop.
"You'll need us one day."
"You'll miss the way we made you feel like Mom was still alive."
"You'll take us with you, won't you?"

She continued to dig.
Her hands grew warm with light.
The violet butterfly paused.

The voices ceased.

She breathed in excitement.

She dug deeper.
Her hands turned hot.

I can't.

"You can," a distant voice giggled.

She continued.

"Breathe, you're safe,"
whispered the violet butterfly.

The light changed to lilac,
revealing a lilac flame flickering deep within.

The butterfly danced.

Another violet butterfly appeared over her right shoulder.

She smiled.

Part VII

The Gifts of Fire: Illuminating the Deeper Mysteries

as above, so below

They say the first witches were the ones to walk away from the
fire to bring back the secrets of shadow.

They were led by their inner spark.

True sight.

They lived in the in-between.

The first daughters of the moon.

Children of night's magick.

With this flame smoldering in her hands, could she illuminate
the gifts she's found?

Fire was always made to guide us deeper into the unknown.

Even the stars of old know this, still leaving remnants of hope
not yet lost to time's darkness.

She holds the lilac flame up to the sky.

She breathes in the voices.

The sky bleeds.

"Mother never loved you."

The lilac flame turned gray.

"You were always going to destroy yourself."

"You're just like her."

The flame grows dim.

The violet butterflies watch.

Her voice quavers.
"My mother didn't know how to love me, but in the end, I know she died wishing she'd known how to all those years ago."

"But she hated you,"
the sky cries.

She looks at the divinity dripping from cracked clouds.
"It's okay to hurt because of what she did to us, but we deserve to move on.
We deserve to heal.
Mother's lies don't have to break us anymore.
We are finding our truths.
And the truth is, even Mother's love now wouldn't save the heartache quaking in our chest. But our own love can rewrite the stars, sending us a reminder that there is always a thread of light if you look for it."

nebulas

_____

Fire starts with energy.

Energy drives action.

Actions can be helpful or harmful.

Fire can keep us warm, but without control,
it will only ever burn.

Fire consumes with passion.

It wards off shadows and embraces light.

It reveals all things.

She clutched the lilac flame close to her heart.

She could feel it dance under her breath, warming her chest.

She had come so far since she set out to make a home
for herself.

It feels like yesterday she was dying in her diary, destined to
destroy dreams desperate to come true.

Now she is basking in flowery meadows, clutching a secret she'd
never knew she'd find.

One she still didn't understand.

Yet she knew it belonged to her.

Fire was her birthright.

bravery was in her voice

_____

In search for the unknown she continues onward,
Using the lilac flame to light the way deeper into her hurts.

The voices remind her of the truths of knives pressed
against her side.

She screams at the sky. "Mother always lies," she cries, kneeling
in the meadow under petals of her soul's earth supporting her
even when she is terrified to stand.

True sight comes from finding a way back home even when
there seems to be only hopelessness ahead.

She closes her eyes and breathes in the constellations of old,
reading the stories weaved from threads of past light lingering
behind.

They'll lead her to what she seeks.

They have to . . .

She stitches her ribs with roses and sunbeams.

She stands in courage.
Her lilac flame grows warmer.

haunted legacies

―――――――

Her heart still holds her abandonment,
Her neglect.
Her punishment.
Her hopelessness.
Her worthlessness.
It was told that's all it ever was.

How desperate she was to feel her mother's hate.
She learned in order to get Mother's love, she'd have to crucify
herself under meadows of lilac skies, wishing she could tell the
difference between a mother's love and a bottle of psych meds.

This is where it began.

Her mother's voice calls the unhealed wounds in her soul
awake.

The fire dims.

believe in what makes your heart glow

Haunted legacies leave behind blood rusted to edges of the heart, still sharp with Mother's touch,

but the fire of truth tears away remnants of shame connecting her to the dead.

The fire of hope melts away regret relived.

The tears won't stop breaking her when she thinks of how she's treated herself since Mom died.

How she became the broken borderline, beating herself to death with the confusion, the sorrow,

and the worthlessness losing a mother who broke you leaves behind, where happily ever afters were supposed to be.

But she's finding a new happily ever after,

one written in forgiveness and curiosity.

The lilac flame grows mauveine.

The butterflies hum nature's hymn.

true sight

Destiny whispers in Fate's ear,
"She's beginning to find the parts of her that bloom eternal."

The stars wade in watery skies, melting colors of wind onto green leaves.

"She is beginning to see beyond life's veil,"
Fate responds, intrigued.

violet

Lilac and mauveine flames flicker in cerulean hues home
to anemones blossoming tenderly among peeking lilacs and
nightingale.

The home inside her chest coursing stardust through her veins
held on even when she couldn't.

She saved herself every time she fell apart.

This is how she puts the pieces back together.

Feeling.

Safety.

Curiosity.

Revelation.

Action.

She offers her soul's compassion to her heart.

She is becoming the haven her hope was waiting for.

The more she heals, the more in love she feels with herself and
with the life she is learning she can choose.

It was always going to be her.

The lilac and mauveine flame glows violet.

From out of the fire, a third butterfly greets her.

She welcomes it like an old friend.

Part VIII

The Gifts of Air: The Breath of Revelation

infinity

_____

I don't want to be my mother anymore,
but who else can I be? she pondered.

lighter than air

Infinite ripples weave their way in and out of time's fairy tale.

The heart finds a way to calm the mind when the heart learns what is worthy of keeping treasured and what is worthy of letting go.

This symbiotic rapport between the mind and the heart are how the soul learns to soften.

CPR

_____

She breathed in sunshine.

She exhaled betrayal.

She'd learned how to sit with herself and melt her fears with self-compassion.

She'd learned how to hold the weight of abandonment riddled with grief trying to grow insidiously inside dreams to make them stillborn.

She'd learned how to resurrect her dead feelings with tender, soft touch.

Her hands that were once razors bloomed divinity, filling the voids trauma left.

Love always stays behind just in case it's needed.

She breathed into the parts of her still trembling.

intertwined

Compassion and patience resurrect the wishes she made in pools of azure under cracked red skies.

Action ignites the soul to stand the test of time's tribulation

Bolts of blueberry skies reveal reveries reforged in raspberry ripples of wind, guiding her heart to the home she seeks.

Destiny smiles.

"I wonder if she knows her power is in how she feels, how she breathes, how she remembers, and how she lets go?"

Fate agrees.

"Perhaps as she remembers, she will learn accepting her hurts is how she lets them go."

The violet flame hums the butterflies' song.

royalty

_____

She breathes love where grief remains.
She knows love will never fully absolve grief.
Grief is love choosing to carry on after them.
This love can bloom beautiful wonders if she wills it.

She'd been broken since she was eight.
Freedom felt wrong when home and abuse felt like the same
thing.

She holds her abandoned parts with soft hands.
The anemones sway in the violet light.
The earth reminds her nature was her mother first.

Destiny asks,
"Do you think she will mother herself how she needed?"

Fate replies,
"I do hope so."

There are so many wonderful things for her to experience if she can only heal by choosing what makes her feel seen,

heard,

wanted by herself.

She's beginning to be the home her dreams need.

Eternity says,

"She'll do it.

It's in her blood."

winters still bloom hope

_____

A letter from Mother Nature.

Dearest little one,

Revelation is stepping into destiny,
holding fate in palms of bravery.
Resilience is the shield of the heart.
The heart is the keeper of the soul.
The soul is hope realized.

It's okay to love yourself whole through every season.
Consistency is how we achieve the wishes our heart makes.

deepening the self

Flashbacks are ripples of memories still trying to find safety.

Guilt calls her name.

Regret bribes her with sinful nothings.

Shame hopes she betrays herself.

She holds the violet flame to the broken pieces of her memories, hoping light shines love into the parts of her starving still for her mother's ghost's approval.

Destiny says,

"In urgency, we find agency."

Fate replies,

"Indeed, sister, this rings true."

untitled vi

———————————

Destiny:

"When the mind is ready, it will choose to remember, hoping the heart can put to rest what tries to bury the soul."

Fate:

"Nevertheless, we still can only heal what we can hold. I hope she learns letting go is a continuum of self-forgiveness and self-acceptance in the present moment. Consistently showing up for ourselves is how we tend to the gardens trying to bloom in sunbeams."

haven of light

She breathes in the voices one more time.

"You aren't ever going to get rid of us," Abandonment screams.

She sits with herself, burning the self-betrayal from her heart.
She'd been trying to please her mother's ghost all her life.
She never knew she could be anything else except her
own demise.

"You won't keep this up. You'll miss us sooner or later and fall
apart just like before. You'll remember how good metal makes
you feel."

She accepts she will have hard days, and there will come times
where the comfortability of the dark may call out to her from
the stain of ghosts no longer there. Still, even then, she will be
there for herself, whatever that means.

A violet butterfly appears.

She remembers.

revelations in a breath of fire

_____

In her memory, she sees something familiar.

she was the gift all along

When she was a little girl, she loved butterflies.

Her favorite color was always violet.

She'd found peace in nature, in its love weathering any season, in how Mother Nature makes homes for all that needed safety.

She'd always longed for a home that stayed.

She never thought she'd be the home for the dreams coming true in front of her eyes.

She'd gained true sight.

She led her heart to the promises she'd tucked away behind violet butterflies, whispering hymns she now understands.

The war was not over,

but she would face the unknown with authority and autonomy.

The adventures she takes from here on out are hers to choose.

a soul's home is the heart

_____

Before the monsters disfigured her nature through nurture,
her heart listened,
her mind knew,
her soul spoke.

She learned broken and falling apart were two different things.

Broken are things that cannot be repaired.
But time does give the possibility for change.
Change does try to grow us where we are still afraid.

She has become the hymn her chest beats.

Happily ever afters still find their way to our doorstep.

Part IX

Letters from beyond the Butterflies

dear older blue i

_____

Dear Older Blue,

Did we ever catch up to the moon? I really tried, reaching up
from the tips of my toes. Did the stars keep our wishes safe? I
told them all my secrets, hoping they'd help us find a happier
place. Are we still looking for a place to belong? Sometimes I
just want to hide away, but do we ever stop feeling lost?

Did we ever start liking it here? I keep hoping it'll feel
like home.

Love,
Younger Blue

dear older blue ii

Dear Older Blue,

Do we ever stop hating ourselves? Do we ever have friends who
don't hurt us? Do we ever feel safe in our body? I want to leave
Mommy, but I'm scared of making Mommy sad and angry. I
just wanted to make our mommy happy. Does she ever stop
hating me? How old is Mommy now?

Do you ever learn to love me?

Love,
Younger Blue

dear older blue iii

_____

Dear Older Blue,

How come I can't remember the things that made me happy?
I like to think I was happy sometimes,
But I only remember Mommy hurting us.
Does she ever stop hurting us?

Sincerely,
Younger Blue

dear younger blue i

———————

Dear Younger Blue,

The moon saves us. The prayers sent in secret for the stars to save us come true.

We make it possible.

We save ourselves from the grave Mother tried to bury us in.

As we heal, we realize Mother was wrong and love was always around us.

Love was always inside us.

Safety was the key to the home holding the hopes you dreamed of, my little one,

hopes life almost made me forget.

Dreams I am beginning to remember I once had.

The more we heal,

the more life shows me happily ever after is mine to choose.

Our little sister passes when we turn twenty-five, and though it breaks us, it catapults us into healing more, especially the relationship with our grandparents, who loved both of us unconditionally. They miss her too. We talk about her sometimes. I know I tell my partner and my friends about her as often as possible because my memory remembers everything about them. I can even remember how they said our name as we'd talk in front of our hallway, sharing stories of the lives we hoped to live once we grew up. We embody them in our values. Patience. Compassion. Empathy. Hope. And vulnerability. We carry them in our poems and letters. We commune with them under the dimly lit moon leading our soul to theirs when the veil thins at magick hour.

Mother never stops hurting us, but we learn how to save and protect our peace. We learn how to set boundaries and how to use our coping skills and our service dog to remind us of the beauty living within us.

Some days, she does pull us from the present, trying to still trap us in the past, but persistence perseveres and lends hope a hand in finding us when we remember how much power we possess simply because we are alive and Mother is not. Self-compassion and empathy heal the cuts still bleeding guilt for her crimes.

It was never our fault.

It was never your fault, little Blue.

I'm sorry I treated you like her all this time.

I do love you.

Sincerely,
Older Blue

dear older blue iv

_____

To Older Blue,

I don't know if this helps your heart,
but I'm happy you stayed to save me.

I forgive you for treating me like Mother.

I'm grateful you chose to save the parts of yourself she tried to kill.

I'm happy you took me away from the monsters.

For what it's worth,
I know you're trying your best.

Sincerely,
Your little Blue

dear older blue v

_____

Older Blue,

It's okay to have fun.

It's okay to fall back in love with yourself.

Flowers always grow big when it's safe.

It's okay to make yourself feel safe.

I'd like that a lot actually.

I've always wanted to know what feeling safe inside feels like.

Love,

Little Blue

dear younger blue ii

_____

Dear Little Blue,

What are some things I can do to help you feel safe?

I promise to be the safe haven you needed then, today, and forever.

Lots of love,
Blue

dear younger blue iii

———————

Dear Younger Blue,

I know your name was filled with lies and hurt from shortcomings of a mother who wasn't fit to love you the way your soul needed to grow.

But I know you.

I see you.

I have traversed time to bestow secret hopes along your way, so when you count the fireflies, you'll feel safe in their illumination.

The stars guided me back to you.

Who knew I would rescue the fragments of my joy, my hope, my tenderness?

Dreams come true through perseverance.

I know this now.

The moon above speaks to this soul below.

Mother's curse won't bind us anymore.

I promise.

Sincerely,
Me

P.S.
I'm so happy I found you again.

dear older blue vi

_____

Dear Older Blue,

You can play more without needing to control or expect anything except for the fun play brings.

Love,
Your little Blue

dear younger blue iv

_____

Dear Little Blue,

I faced the monsters for you.

I learned to bloom wildflowers and lilacs from my tears because I learned to face the monsters.

I learned to stare at bolts of blue hiding starlight, waiting for the moon to rise and feel in awe again.

I learned love isn't trying to be perfect,

it is loving the parts of you no one else sees.

It is accepting the shadows when they try to speak and listening to their cries as prayers for help.

I learned the monsters of the past can heal in the warmth of the present, if only I will it.

Thank you for reminding me of my strength.

I'm strong because I never want to let you down again.

Forever and always,

Me

dear older blue vii

_____

Dear Blue,

It makes me happy you love me.

I love you too.

I'm so happy it was you who found me instead of the scary monsters

that ask for things I no longer want to give.

You rescued me like I always knew you would.

I'm home.

Sincerely,
Your little Blue

Dear stars,
Thank you for guiding Blue back to me.

Sincerely,
Your little Blue

dear younger blue v

Who would have thought, little Blue, that we would have found happily ever after in the way we learned to show up for each other?

How I learned how to listen to your needs, and you learned it was safe to express the things your heart needed?

I'm grateful hope never dies.

I'm grateful love persists after death.

I'm grateful light leads dreams to my windowsill.

Who would have thought that one day, I would sit in the quiet of redwood trees, listening to old sparrows sing the songs of timeless forests and think how all this time, you kept hoping I'd save you?

Me.

Us.

Who would have thought that one day, we would learn how to live life so both of us enjoy it.

Little Blue, you deserve to accomplish the dreams Mother took from you.

As above,

So below.

Finding you has made life beautiful.

My soul sees beyond the butterflies into the home waiting for me.

For us.

Sincerely,

Blue

P.S. We achieve everything our mother said we couldn't and wouldn't do.

Life loves having you in it.